I0699265

meet me between breaths

J. P. Greene

Meet Me Between Breaths
by J.P. Greene

Copyright © 2024 Joshua Paul Greene

Published by **Tape Publishing**, 2025

This book was set in 11 pt Goudy Old Style

10 9 8 7 6 5 4 3 2

Printed in the United States of America on acid-free paper. For information write to hello@typewrittenlovenotes.com

ISBN 979-8-9913038-1-1

First Paperback Edition

PUBLISHER'S NOTE:
This is a work of fiction. Names, characters, places, and incidents either are the product of the author's imagination or are used fictitiously, and any resemblance to actual persons, living or dead, events, or locales is entirely coincidental.

Cover photograph by Sean Benesh, used under license from Unsplash.com. Cover design and book layout by the author.

Since you kissed me
my mouth can only
speak in poems.

For my kids —

May you find the kind of love
that makes you believe in yourself.

—

What you're about to read is more than a poetry collection. While it is, essentially, a collection of poems with a few short stories scattered throughout, it's meant to be read front to back, like a novel. This is the story of Lorenzo and Eleanore, their uncommon love for one another, and their unconventional relationship. I hope you enjoy reading these two as much as I've enjoyed writing them.

— Josh

meet me between breaths

Friday night dates
soft new lips
the thrill of
foreign smiles
or an electric
caress from a hand
I've never held.

But damn if it
wouldn't be nice
to really be
in love
again.

I

Music was coming through from the apartment upstairs. Lorenzo was reclined on his bed in his pants and an undershirt, his arms crossed beneath his head. In one corner of the room, a record spun on a player as gypsy jazz tunes from the days of Django Reinhardt did their best to compete with the drum and bass bleeding through the plaster ceiling from the neighbor's party.

Behind his head the window was open to the rainy evening outside, and the smell of the wet air and late spring drifted in scented with magnolia blooms. He stared up at the ceiling, at the conical drape of amber lent by the side table lamp, and listened to the sounds of cars on the road out of sight, their tires like tides of static washing across the wet asphalt.

When the record ran out, he rose, lifted the needle, and paused in place, listening to the incessant music from elsewhere in the building. He glanced at the clock in the kitchen that he could barely see through the doorway. It was 11:11 in the evening. Sunday night. He stood, thinking for a few more moments, and then went out.

Upstairs in the hallway, he waited outside the door to apartment 405 with one forearm resting against the jamb and his other hand holding his whiskey glass by the top rim. He waited. The noise reverberated through the walls more clearly than it had in his apartment, and from where he now stood he could hear the adornments of laughter and conversation overtop of the music. After a minute or so with no answer he knocked once more, and then tried the knob. The door opened.

Inside he found the room dimly lit, people scattered here and there, a neon sign that said *Las Vegas* buzzing pink and blue into the hazy dark. On the sofa just inside the front door were two college-aged individuals passing a purple glass bong between them and half-watching *Lock, Stock and Two Smoking Barrels*. One of them looked up without interrupting his hit and watched Lorenzo cross the room. Nobody spoke.

In the kitchen, through the smoke and the throb of the music, Lorenzo could see a man fishing limes out of the garbage disposal. He crossed to him and asked if he knew whose place it was. The man nodded, tossed a handful of lime wedges into the open trashcan beside the sink, and pointed one dripping finger toward the open window. Lorenzo thanked him and wove his way through the dancing people.

Outside, the rain had slowed to a drizzle. The window was double-hung, tall and narrow, and made of the same wavy original glass as the rest of the windows in the 1920's apartment building. The wooden sill stood only about a foot off the floor, and beyond it he could see a fire escape platform floored by an iron grate, with a painted iron railing running the perimeter. On the ascending flight of steps, a girl was sitting leaned back on her elbows. She was staring over her shoulder at the darkness beyond and shifted her gaze toward the window when Lorenzo appeared. She smiled at him but did not speak. He paused, and then climbed through, standing thereafter on the platform with his hands awkwardly at his sides, the one still holding his now-nearly-empty glass.

After a moment he took a cigarette from behind his ear and placed it between his lips. Patting his pockets, he realized he didn't have a lighter. The girl extended one long, slender arm with a tarnished brass Zippo held easily between her thumb and forefinger. She had tattoos on her hands that disappeared beneath the sleeves of an oversized sweatshirt, and she looked pleased with herself.

Thanks, he said, watching her eyes, their gaze unbroken as he took the lighter, lit his cigarette, snapped shut the lid, and handed it back. Who are you? she asked.

He chuckled to himself. Lorenzo. Who are *you?*

She looked to her left. Depends who's asking, she said.

This your place?

I'm not at liberty to say, she replied wistfully, her face turning back toward him.

You're a terrible liar.

Guilty, she said. Her eyes were like embers in the night.

Isn't it a bit late for a party, he said then, taking a drag on his cigarette.

Didn't you know? It's never too late for a party. Parties are all the rage these days.

He nodded slowly, as though just now understanding.

Besides, parties are a wonderful way to meet interesting new people.

And that's why you're out here all alone, is it? he asked flatly.

Well, it's lured you here, hasn't it?

He exhaled a plume of smoke into the night. I don't think you'll find me very interesting.

Why don't you leave that to me to decide?

Suit yourself, he replied.

Eleanore, the girl said.

What? he asked.

My name is Eleanore.

That's a beautiful name, he said, extending his hand.

Isn't it though?

He looked at her, half-smiling, and she scrunched up the corners of her eyes. It is, he said.

When they released, he leaned his forearms against the wetted railing and she resumed her study of the humid dark. He found himself silently wondering what it would sound like if he dropped his glass and it fell to the pavement below.

It would be satisfying, wouldn't it?

He turned his head.

To drop the glass, she continued.

He stared at her.

Need another drink? she asked without waiting for him to respond. She rose and stood beside him. I shouldn't, he said.

Why not? she asked. What else have you got to do tonight?

Sleep, he thought. Or a million other things besides falling in love. Alright, he said. Just one.

She smiled coyly at him and took his glass from his hand, and then she disappeared through the window. Because of the darkness outside it was easy to see into the apartment but he didn't watch her. He could see the city skyline beyond the rise and fall of a few hills, some blanketed with lawns and parks, others crossed with a patchwork of boulevards and streets and buildings. The city shimmered against the drizzly sky.

And then she had returned, standing beside him and handing back his glass. Instead of resuming her seat on the fire escape stairs, though, she remained standing, she herself resting her arms on the railing. Her sweatshirt fell down one arm, exposing her shoulder. She was close enough that their arms brushed here and there, and close enough to whisper and still be heard.

It's not a bad view, he said.

Can I take your picture? she asked after a moment. He let the whiskey in his mouth go down, feeling it burn his throat pleasantly. If you want, he replied.

Must get heavy –
the way she carries
every gaze in the room.

Maybe that's why
she's got such
nice legs.

Who knew
sight of a shoulder
could ruin a man
for life.

Got lost in her eyes
hit my teeth with my glass
she laughed
with her whole body
blinded me with
her radiance
and I lost my heart
forever.

J.P. Greene

Did you know
eyes across
a crowded room
can ignite a blast
so powerful you'll
find clothes all
over the house?

Just... what if
we were in love
and it was okay
that you took up
every inch of space
in my mind and when
I kissed you goodnight
it meant forever,
instead of goodbye.

I find myself
wanting to explore
every crevice of
the universe with you.
Which is to say
I wonder what
it might be like
if we fell in love.

Wouldn't it be nice
to hold your hand
under the breakfast table.

Does the moon know
her gravity pulls
every gaze on earth?

Do you know
yours does too?

Someone asked:
How are you doing?

I said I was starving.

But what I meant is
I'm desperate
to know all of
everything about
you.

How intimate it is
he thinks
to sleep with someone
so that when you stir
they rouse and touch you
and then you both fall
back asleep together.

I could fall for you
you know…

It would be easy
to slip on your smile
reach for your hand
fall into your eyes
while you help me
to stand and never again
set a foot onto land
and it would all feel
as natural as breathing.

I could fall for you
and it would be as
effortless as
believing in
gravity.

I love you
is currently caught
between this
boundless heart
and the part of me
that knows I only
met you five
minutes ago.

Wouldn't it be nice
if your voice
became the lullaby
I hear every night
just before falling
asleep.

II

He stood on the fire escape smoking and looking out at the midday sun, feeling it land across his face, warm against the unseasonable chill in the air. It's too cold for May, he was thinking. But the sun felt nice. It was Saturday.

As the smoke climbed upwards like a silk thread connecting heaven and earth, he wondered about Eleanore, whom he hadn't seen since the night nearly a week ago when they met. He looked upward to where her fire escape platform jutted directly above his, and wondered then how he'd never seen her out there before. He pulled from his back pocket a small notebook and jotted down a few lines, then replaced it and took one last drag on the cigarette.

When he went out an hour later it was without any particular destination in mind. He just had that sort of feeling that made him want to be in the city walking, and so he parked by the stadium and took the pedestrian bridge over the river and walked up the streets looking in the windows. Up a ways on Second he saw a vintage shop and turned in through the barred glass door. The woman behind the counter looked up and smiled and he replied with a Hello and proceeded to amble through the densely arranged rooms piled with all manner of old and mostly useless things. On the far side of the store about halfway back he came to an old wooden Mission style armoire with its doors removed, the shelves inside containing several old manual typewriters. Most of them were very large, heavy desktop models from the twenties, thirties and forties – an Underwood, one Mercedes – but there was one 1960's Olivetti Lettera 32 in teal among them that captured his attention immediately. He pulled a scrap of receipt paper from his pocket, threaded it through, and typed a few test lines. The action was smooth and responsive, the report of the keys on the paper whisper quiet, the progression of the carriage immediate and precise. He examined the ribbon and the keys themselves and the feet for each letter, picked it up to feel its weight, looking at it from all sides. Then he brought it to the front, purchased it, and went out.

It didn't have a case, so he carried it under his arm as he continued to walk back through the city, tourists occasionally looking at him, probably because of his flat cap and typewriter, as though he were himself some transplant from another time and some charming part of this city in which so many were only visitors.

The typewriter was heavy and he found himself wanting for a drink, so he stopped in The Atlantic on lower Broadway for a whiskey and soda. The Atlantic was a nice place in the daylight with flooring made of small, white hexagonal tiles set with charcoal grout, its bar white granite, and the barback a long, tarnished mirror, adorned with amber bottles of liquor. The fixtures were of wood or pewter metal, and with the typewriter and his cap and his penchant for things long forgotten, he could've been a Norman Rockwell painting, except for his unruly, curly dark hair.

The bartender brought his drink and commented on the typewriter. Thanks, Lorenzo said, I just bought it. Haven't even had a chance to work it yet.

You want a piece of paper or something? the bartender asked. Lorenzo said yes, if he wouldn't mind. The man disappeared into the back and returned with a few sheets of printer paper and set them on the bar. Lorenzo thanked him and threaded the first page through the roller, dropped the bail bar and set his margins. Well, he said to the page – though he was actually talking to the bartender – with what words shall I christen this beautiful machine?

Well, what'd you buy it to write?

Poetry, mostly. But I'm working on a novel, too. I've got an old fifties Smith-Corona portable that I've been writing on, but this one's smoother. It'll be faster going.

Poetry, huh? Like love poems or something?

Something like that, he said.

Well, you got a girl?

Lorenzo took a drink of his whiskey soda, looking at the other man over the top of the glass as he tipped it. He swallowed, set it down, exhaled.

Maybe write about her then.

He looked at the page. The sun was streaming through the window and landing in bars that shimmered as the cars passed outside, and for a moment he thought how much he liked having a drink in the middle of the day. It was a still, slow luxury, one of those things that seemed always to demark very good days, and it wasn't even the intoxication that followed the drink that he liked, but the way it slipped leisurely into the folds of his life and made space among so many busy things.

The door opened and a beverage salesman walked in with cases of liquor on a dolly. The door closed behind him and Lorenzo went back to looking at his blank page. Eleanore, he thought. He typed a few words, studied them, hit the carriage return and typed another line. In a few minutes he had finished and he fed the paper all the way out, then ran it through backwards to straighten the bend from the roller. He placed it face-up on the bar and weighted it with his glass, then fed the second paper through the machine, eyeballed the margins to center the type, adjusted the set brackets, and duplicated the poem. Once it was finished he spooled it out, ran it through in reverse, and set it down on the bar beside the first one.

Two of em, eh? the bartender asked from a ways down the bar where he stood polishing some glasses.

Yeah, Lorenzo replied. One for me, one for you. You can frame it and put it up. Tell em all you know me one day when I'm famous. You got a pen?

The bartender smiled and slid one down the bar. A nice pen with a steel barrel and a smooth cartridge. Lorenzo twisted it, signed the page below the poem in his swooping, elegant signature, with the L that encircled the rest of the letters, and twisted the pen closed. A Lorenzo Matorri original, he said, winking.

The bartender came down the bar, picked it up, and read it.

You just came up with this? Just now? In just those few minutes it took?

Lorenzo finished his drink, set it down, and nodded. Be easy on me, he said. You don't have to frame it.

Man, the bartender said. This is really something. You got it bad for this girl don't you.

Lorenzo half-smiled, pulling a twenty from his pocket.

The bartender was re-reading the poem and didn't answer.

Lorenzo folded the bill long-ways and set it down on the bar.

The bartender waved his hand and shook his head but didn't stop reading the poem. Lorenzo figured it was probably the fifth time he'd read it. No, he said. This one's on me. This here's worth more than that drink and a hundred more. Tell you what, you come in here anytime and tell em you wrote this poem – and I do plan on putting it up on that wall back there – and you got drinks on the house.

I couldn't, Lorenzo answered. I'll take the one today. But I have to support my favorite spots. It's a non-negotiable. And if you won't take the money, I'll hide it around the place. Don't think I won't.

The bartender smiled again, finally put the paper carefully inside a binder which he returned to a shelf behind the bar and extended his hand. Nick, he said.

Lorenzo – Pleasure to meet you, Nick. And thanks for the drink.

The pleasure is mine, Nick said.

Lorenzo put his cap back on, picked up the typewriter, and nodded one last time before heading for the door.

When he got back to his building, he found Eleanore sitting on the front steps, leaning back, the same way he'd found her the first night on her fire escape.

She smiled as he approached, crinkling the corners of her eyes, looking up at him. Where have you been? she asked. And what is that? She waggled her index finger at the typewriter held in his arm.

Hello, he said. Eleanore. She was the most beautiful girl he'd ever seen.

You didn't answer my question.

It's a typewriter.

I can see that, she said. She hadn't moved. What's it for?

Typing, he said.

She rolled her eyes.

He smiled. Poetry. And novels.

On that thing? You're joking.

It would be more efficient if I was, he replied.

She smiled again at him. Then she got up, brushed off the back of her pants, and put her hands in her pockets.

Where are you off to, he asked.

Coming with you, she said.

Oh, well by all means. Lead the way.

She danced up the steps, her hair bouncing as she did so, and opened the door, which she held for him. He walked inside and began climbing the stairs.

Inside his apartment he closed the door behind her and set the typewriter down on the table. She looked around casually, walking the floor and looking closely but in a serene sort of way at the pictures and items and books that lined the shelves and surfaces around the apartment.

Well, she said, still looking around. Are you going to read to me?

He watched her but didn't speak.

She looked across the room at him, the last of the day's sun filtering through the sheer curtains which hung from curtain rods over each of the tall windows. Dust hung mid-air and glittered like gold, the haze of late afternoon making the image of her into a faded polaroid of a moment. Don't move, he told her. She obeyed, she herself stilled like the golden dust in the sunlight. He picked up an old Canon 35mm camera, progressed the film, adjusted the settings, and clicked a few shots. She was half-smiling at him in both.

Now we're even, he said.

I hope it doesn't stay that way, she replied. I like a bit of play. Can I move yet, sir? She looked at him very seriously from the tops of her eyes.

He was replacing the lens cap. I'll allow it, he said. She bit her lip involuntarily but he didn't see this as he set the camera down. So you want me to read to you, he added, looking through a pile of papers on an old, weathered writing table beside his Smith-Corona.

Yes, she said, now thumbing through his vinyl records.

He extracted a stack of papers bound with a crude manuscript binding and seated himself on the sofa. She was looking at the label on the record currently on the turntable, and after a moment she nodded, crossed to him, and sat down very close, leaning up against him and resting her head on his shoulder. What are you going to read to me? she asked.

... but what if
I love you and
it lasts forever?

To sit in silence
with you, or to hold
your hand, or to
touch your leg in the car.

To just be beside you
and to wonder what
it would be like to
love you...

or to wonder
if maybe I already do.

Because maybe I already do.

Just kiss her
he thought.

You've both
damn well
wanted it
long enough.

Thinking of you has
become as simple
and effortless
as breathing.

Take pictures of me
she said
so I can see me
the way you do.

But she's so much more
than shadows and light
and skin and bone.

And what I love most
are all the things
you'd never guess
just by looking at her.

Finally home.

I lay down.

The clock says
it's tomorrow.

But my body says
You expect
me to sleep?

After a kiss
like that?

My mind wanders
all day long
over the unfamiliar
terrain that is
you.

Don't kiss and tell
they say
but they've never
met God on the lips
of a stranger
the way I did
with you.

Some girls send nudes.

She sent me poetry
so obviously
I fell in love.

We met in the spring
and my heart bloomed
along with so many
flowers.

Thoughts of you
pepper the sky
of my mind
like a million
tiny birds urged
from their trees
by the earth-shaking
arrival of you
in my life.

Maybe one day
when it has become
endearing that I
loved you from the
first moment we met,
I'll show you
all the poems I've
written.

They'll be ones
you've already seen
but for the first time
you'll realize
they were all
about you.

She kissed me and
I lost all need
for words.

For the first time
my lips had a
whole new way
to say
I love you.

Let's get drunk
on the porch in a
rainstorm
make love in tall grass
wet through and through
as the thunder crashes
and the lightning illuminates
your eyes and mine and
our bodies entwined
and the whole world
barreling on
beautiful and gruesome
and ours for the taking.

But I don't really want
the world.

I just want you.

III

Around them swirled the hushed conversations and the tinkle of silverware on fine plates, and as the table-top alcohol lamp flickered between them she watched the way it reflected off the glass of his eyes. He watched her without saying anything. She smiled, tucked a strand of hair behind her ear, and shifted her chin down and to the side, looking at him from the tops of her eyes, and fluttered her eyelashes.

The things you do to me, he said.

What, she asked, smiling and rearranging her place setting.

Like you don't know.

What things?

Oh... The looking at me like you love me, for example.

I've always been a lousy liar.

So, you do, then. Love me.

She smiled that same way like she had a secret she almost couldn't bear to keep, but didn't respond.

You're thinking about something.

She looked at him then, falling into his eyes for a moment before she was able collect herself again, drew a breath, and said she'd been meaning to tell him something.

Well, he said. Go on.

The waiter brought their drinks, set them on the table, and receded without either of them breaking their gaze.

I was looking at some of the pictures we've taken, last night while you were writing.

Mhmm, he said, eyeing her with a curious, almost sly expression.

And I just... Lorenzo - she smoothed the folds of her dress across the tops of her thighs - We're very beautiful together.

He swallowed and set his drink back on the table. I've noticed, he said. And then he smiled.

I know you're not wild about the auto shop.

I don't mind it, he interjected. I like working with my hands. I like the problem-solving.

But what if you could just write, she said, looking at him.

He stared at her with a very serious expression.

Wouldn't you prefer that? she asked.

I mean - you know how I feel about art burdened by income, he said.

Yes, I know, she said. I'm not... This isn't about making a living off of your writing.

What are you after? he asked, squinting at her as though her proposition was a very dubious one. He was relaxed in his seat. She was leaning forward with her elbows on the table.

The waiter returned and asked if they were ready to order food.

Surprise us, Lorenzo said, and handed him their menus. She's allergic to shellfish. The waiter nodded and went away.

For a moment that seemed to suspend itself in time, Eleanore looked at him and he looked at her and everything seemed so very simple somehow.

Lorenzo, she said again, looking at him earnestly. We're very beautiful. We could do something with that.

He studied her face. You think that could work? he asked. He lifted the Luxardo cherry on its wooden skewer from his glass and, holding his other hand beneath it, palm up, reached it across the table to her. She carefully took it between her teeth, and he removed the spear all without either of them looking away from the other.

She smiled as she chewed and nodded her response to his previous question.

Enough money to live on? he asked after a moment of silence. And she nodded again.

How much?

She nearly chuckled. Based on what I've been learning... Twenty.

Thousand?

At least.

A year?

A devious light flickered in her eyes and she looked at him coyly. She shook her head.

A month?

She smiled but neither said nor indicated anything else with her body language.

Eleanore. You can't be serious.

Oh, darling – I am.

He frowned and ran his thumb and forefinger around the topography of the cut glass tumbler in which his drink had been. Then he looked at her. Around them life went on as usual but within him everything was changing.

She had shifted such that her legs were crossed, her left arm across the back of her chair. She had curled her hair in a sort of modern-looking finger wave and the fine straps and low cut of her dress did a fair justice to her beautiful chest and neck. He paused on the shadows that pooled in the hollows of her collarbones and paused, too, appreciating the way her shoulders came together to frame her architecture.

Tell me more, he said after a moment.

I would want it to be in the style of the photographs we've taken already. Very many of them we could use. I would like them to be on film, very tasteful, and I would like a combination of photos of just you, and just me, and of us together, obviously. And I would like to include some of other women with us.

Lorenzo nodded and sipped off the full drink the waiter had just brought. I think you're more beautiful than I am, he said. I don't know about the other women.

That's what makes you so gorgeous, she replied. It's in your eyes. This humility. It's almost sad. I was seeing it in the photographs I was looking at last night. It kept capturing me somehow.

You think I look sad? he chuckled.

No, not sad. That's not the right word. Tortured isn't right either. Stoic? It just appears as though you're going to get on with life no matter the cost. It comes across as strength. But it forms your face and it's very, very beautiful.

You're very, very beautiful.

We both are.

The waiter brought their food and explained what each of the plates held and when they had been informed, he left them alone.

Okay, Eleanore, Lorenzo said, laying his napkin across his lap.

Okay? she asked across the table, looking at him like she was waiting for him to say more.

Okay, he said again. And he gave her that look that melted everything else away and he smiled the sort of smile that had always made her certain that he was exactly the person she thought he was. That he was, truly, the person she had always wanted, the person she loved, and the person she was meant to end up with.

Okay, she said. And she gathered a forkful of pasta and smiled to herself.

But, he said, I want some pictures just for me.

Anything you want, she replied, still smiling.

Sometimes when
we're together
I forget to breathe.

It's not that you
take my breath away...

More like my body
feels so complete
in your presence
I'm not sure I
could ever need
anything else.

Is it too much to ask
just to be touching
you every second for
the rest of my life?

If we're quiet enough
do you think we'll
be able to hear
our hearts
whispering?

...the kind of love
where her morning eyes
become the sunrise
to start my every day.

Can't for the life
of me remember
what I thought about
all day

before you.

Be careful
with those eyes
that could drag out
every secret in my soul
or I might slip and say
I love you.

Like a lake
reflecting the stars
back at the soft
navy sky,

I get the sense
our eyes have been
conversing for
much longer than
time has even
existed.

I was trying to figure
out what it was about
holding your hand on
that snowy street that
felt so special.

Then I realized it
was you.

It's always
just been you.

She was a very good
influence in that she
got him out of the
house and out of his
head, and that there
was something about
her he fell in love
with every day, and
when he was in love
he held the world
more tenderly and after
a time it began to seem
that all the flowers
bloomed so that he
could pick them and
give them to her and
it seemed that he
himself bloomed because
she had given herself
to him.

Look at these hearts
of ours beating
like they've never
been broken.

IV

They had finished making love and were lying together on the precipice of sleep. The shadows hung against the brick walls and high ceilings like the dark itself was at rest.

Lorenzo, she said. Her voice was soft and small, like he could put it in his pocket and keep it there forever without it ever getting in the way. They were on his bed, a slideshow of headlights passing along the crown molding, brightening the room in amber hues and then fading back to the deep velvet blue known most intimately to the early hours of the morning. He didn't respond, except to tilt his head so that his chin nuzzled the crown of hers. Mmm, he said after a moment drifting contentedly in half-sleep. Everything was still.

She was silent; he waited. After another car had passed, its sound dissipating down the street, she said: There's something I want to tell you. Her words were soft and round and gentle, and she might not have even been fully awake. As though, in the morning she might not remember any of it at all. But he knew hers were conscious words.

He waited.

You— she swallowed. She was very sleepy.

I just have to tell you, that I am in love with you. I know we haven't really said that yet. But. It's true. I am.

She said it like she was reading the lines from a storybook. Like there was nothing careful or cautious about them. Just a matter-of-fact statement in a soft, sleepy voice laced with the hint of a smile.

In the dark he stared at the ceiling and prayed for a car to pass and then wondered why he had wanted that. Words welled up inside him but died before he could wrench open his mouth to speak them. They were words she'd spoken so lightly but it felt to him as though they carried so much weight. Like they carried an expectation or like they waited for his response. It felt like he would drown in the silence.

But there was nothing. No crashing wave. No blood. No retreat or resentment. Just the warm rise and fall of her breathing and the effortless weight of her head on his chest and her hand heavy with sleep on his stomach. It was as simple as if she'd said it a thousand times. And the comfortable stillness made him feel worse.

He kissed her head then and closed his eyes, and she pressed almost imperceptibly closer to him, and then they both drifted off together.

When she came into his apartment late in the afternoon of the next day, expecting to see him there at his desk, writing, or reclined against the escape railing reading a book, she found the whole place still. Light pooled on the floor – late, deep orange puddles – the windows open, or maybe just one, down in the corner of the room. On his desk sat his typewriter – the Smith-Corona – and in it, a paper. It rustled stiffly in the slight breeze that drifted in from the window. For a moment she stood just inside the doorway, her keys slack in her hands, her bag and her flannel hanging off her shoulder, her legs crossed at the ankle, looking. Then she crossed to the desk, setting down her things on the kitchen table on the way, dropping the flannel to the floor in a heap, and looked at the paper. It had her name at the top.

She paused, her throat tight and her eyes burning. And then she read:

Eleanore—

What do you do with a man
who writes poems
that bring people to tears
but can't speak the words
I love you.

There's an image of me
that screams tenderness and
flows with words like flowers
and everybody thinks that I
live with this blooming
fragrant heart.

But when it came down to it
in the deep of a night that could've
easily turned into the rest of my life
I hit a wall and fell silent.

A lifeless animal crumpled
still warm from the effort
of running.

Your voice rang out
in the quiet room
like a gunshot, your words as
visible as steam on a mirror
and I lay there beneath you like

I was being suffocated when really
you were weightless
and I was the one holding the gun.

I'm a bird too scared to fly
when the cage door opens
not because I don't trust it
but because I am broken.

And I'm scared that if I give
my heart I'll panic and in
my manic flutter I'll break
your hollow bones.

But they're not hollow.
The only thing fragile
is me.

When she finished reading, she pulled it from the
typewriter and held it gently and simply between her
thumbs and forefingers and she gazed out the window
at a branch floating in the breeze, the leaves rustling.
Then she fished a receipt from her pocket, fed it
through the typewriter, sat down in the chair, and
typed:

Lorenzo –

Love lives beyond words
in the space between breaths.

That's where we met
and where we will live
forever.

She paused, her fingers hovering over the keys of the typewriter. And then she relaxed her pose, resting her hands in her lap, and looked over her shoulder. Only then did she notice him watching her from the doorway. She smiled sweetly at him. And he continued to lean his shoulder into the door jamb, both his hands in his pockets. Will you have me? he asked.

She stayed where she was, watching him, and nodded, still smiling.

He wouldn't find the receipt paper in the typewriter until the next morning, when he sat down in the grey light of five A.M. to write while the birds chirped though the open window. And when he found it, he looked to where he could see the corner of the bed through the open bedroom doorway, early shadows in the sleeping apartment, and he smiled, rose, and crawled back into bed next to her. He threaded his arm beneath hers, across her chest, his leg topping her leg. She pressed back into him and in this way they slept until ten. And when they woke, it was raining.

Our first date
we sat in the rain
and watched evening
fall.

And I knew then
even if all the world
came down around us
we'd still have
smiles on our faces.

I guess the sky
and I both fell
for you that night.

Isn't it nice
the way these
thoughts of you
lift my spirits
feet floating
inches above the
ground and all
my horizons new
again?

When we talk
you and I
in the still depth
of moonlit nights
every word we share
becomes a star
that will shine
through every other darkness
for the rest
of my life.

They lay there
together on the hood
of the car and he said
I want to see
a shooting star.

A while later they
saw one and he wondered
what else he might
have if he were to
have the courage
to ask for it.

So he took her hand
and she didn't let go
that night
or ever.

I'd say she put
stars in my eyes
but the truth is
she filled me
with a whole
damn galaxy.

I touched her leg
under the table
right above the knee
my fingertips teasing
the hem of her dress
and she lost her words
and looked at me
and I thought...

These kinds of fireworks
shouldn't be allowed
inside.

Kiss me awake
so I can spend
another Sunday
loving you.

The way you're
the first thought
on my mind when
I open my eyes
even if I was
just blinking.

Some people take
a little cream
or sugar with
their coffee,
but I prefer a
few drops of sun
and a brief
eternity of your
body melting
into mine.

She kisses like
her lips could
save the world.

Sometimes I overhear
my hands and my eyes
and my heart
whispering on and on
about how beautiful
you are.

We must choose
to love with abandon
or to abandon love.

There is no middle ground
in matters of the heart.

Still searching
for the stars I saw
when she kissed me.

I wouldn't mind
feeling under the
weather if the
weather was you.

I got lost
somewhere between
your eyes
and the inside
of your thighs.

Don't send help.

I'm fine here
wherever I am.

She was a lesson
in gravity
or momentum
or whatever it is
that makes one body
feel like colliding
with another.

V

It had been a very late flight, and it was already past one in the morning when they arrived at the hotel and the front desk had given them a heavy brass key for the door to their room. When they got up to the room and unlocked and opened the door, they found the queen bed made with white sheets and a mustard orange bedspread, and a table lamp switched on beside it. They entered and put down their things and then he crossed the room and slid open the window to vent the space with the cool, wet air blowing in from the ocean to the west. It was August and very hot, even after dark, and even though it seemed like it might rain.

She had gone into the bathroom and was re-applying her lipstick in the mirror. He came to stand behind her, his hands on her hips, which she pushed slightly toward him. Their eyes met in the mirror. Are you tired? she asked him. Not as much as I should be for the hour, he answered. She twisted the lipstick down and replaced its cap, and turned to face him, resting her hands on his chest. My little old man, she said affectionately.

Do you still want to go out? she asked after they had kissed for a few seconds.

I could, he said.

Not very convincing, she mused, smiling and breaking away.

What if we stayed in, he said over his shoulder as he looked in the mirror at a spot on his neck just below his jaw where he had missed with the razor.

Will you read me something? she asked. She had seated herself on the bed and was loosening the buckles on the ankle straps of her heels. The dress she was wearing was split up the side nearly to her hip and he watched the long line of her bare leg as she did this.

You're always wanting for me to read to you, he said, his voice playfully intoned with resistance.

She looked up then and smiled. Only if you want to, she said.

I always want to, he responded.

Read me the bit you were writing on the plane, she said then. He was leaning against the bathroom doorway, his tie undone now and hanging from his shirt collar, the top two buttons of his shirt open.

That tragic bit? he asked.

She smiled again – seemed always to be smiling – and nodded. Yeah – where we left off.

He went for his bag, unclasped it, and pulled out the pages. Then he sat on the bed and leaned up against the headboard and flipped through the manuscript until he came to the section she had requested. She shifted herself up beside him and nestled down in the hem of his arm. As he began to read, she casually, with one hand, worked loose the remaining buttons on his shirt and stroked his chest sweetly and absentmindedly. As he read through the pages, he could feel the muscles in her face contract into a smile at the parts she liked most, and he would often play with the strands of her hair that fell on her shoulder, or finger the satin strap of her dress. After a time, he could tell by the rhythmic rise and fall of her breathing that she had fallen asleep.

Carefully, so as not to wake her, he reached over and set the manuscript on the side table next to the bed, and then maneuvered her so that she was laying on her stomach. When he rose, she asked in half-sleep where he was going. I'll be right back, he said. She asked if he would undress her, which he did tenderly, and she wiggled herself beneath the covers.

When she was back asleep, he went out of the room and down the hall to the door to the fire escape, where he sat on the railing and smoked a cigarette. It was raining now and he could see the drops catching fleeting glints of the streetlights and traffic lights and the headlights of a few passing cars. While he smoked, he thought about the failures of men in general and about all the ways he had failed in particular. He thought it a cruel reality that no matter how many good things he did it was still the blind, fumbling mistakes he remembered most pointedly and in the greatest detail. He blew his last puff out in a soft pillar of grey against the deep softness of the night and stubbed the cigarette out on the fire escape railing.

When he came back into the room, he saw that she hadn't moved. He crossed quietly to the bathroom where he washed his hands and brushed his teeth. Then he shed his clothes, turned out the lights, and climbed into bed beside her. As she did every night when he came to bed, she turned so her back was toward him and pressed her body against his. And as he did every night when she did this, he worked one arm beneath her pillow and the other around her so that his top hand held her chest just between her breasts. She found his top hand with hers and slid her fingers between his and then she pressed herself against him again.

Sometimes they would make love like this and sometimes it was such sleepy lovemaking that they would fall asleep with him still inside her. But other times, as on this night at 2:07 in the morning in a very old hotel room in a city by the sea that was not their own, they simply fell asleep holding each other, each of them knowing that no matter what mistakes plagued their consciousness, they had found somewhere to call home, and they had found it in each other.

Isn't it fun
to live this way?

Let's stay young
and beautiful
forever.

Until her
I was not aware
that lips have the power
to stop time
completely.

How about
this Sunday
we do that
other thing
that makes us
both call out
God's name?

It's amazing that
something as soft
as your lips can
leave a permanent
dent in my memory.

I want to know if your lips
taste better on a rainy street
or beneath the swirl of a snowy
porchlight or on a cliff over
the sea where the salt joins in
or if they really do taste best
anywhere and everywhere as long
as your body's against mine
and my hands are in your hair.

She was every
sweet poem
about summer
I'd ever heard.

The way your body
fits with mine
is a very underrated
magic.

I think the way
you know who you
love is that,
sometimes it feels
like settling to be
with someone, and
sometimes it feels
like settling to
have to live
without them.

Most poems
are shit
compared
to her.

Your eyes are
asking questions
my lips know how
to answer without
speaking a word...

Kiss my neck
nibble my ear
and you will
discover my
fondness for
pulling hair.

I think I'd like
to go traveling
she said.

Just so I can kiss you
in other places I've
loved you in all the
lifetimes before this one.

They stood
the two of them
looking out over
the glittering expanse
and he felt sad for the
beauty of the world
because it would never
live up to the way
she moved him.

...difficult to speak
when all my lips
want to do is
kiss you...

Whatever magic seems
to have scooped us up
I'm here for it.

Just...
let me savor the scent
of morning sun on your neck
a little while longer.

Probably I can't keep
my hands off you
whenever we're together
because my soul
has had enough of existing
half within me and
half within you
and so it schemes
with every inch of skin
trying desperately to
make us collide once
and for all.

When we come together
and slip off the edge
of the world.

VI

When she awoke, he was already sitting out on the balcony with his back against the railing and the bottom case of his Smith-Corona portable typewriter resting on his legs, which were crossed at the ankles. He was wearing the black-framed glasses that she always said made him look very serious, a plain white T-shirt, and the same pair of navy slacks he'd had on the night before. Beside him sat his usual accompaniments: a glass of water, no ice; a tumbler glass of whiskey, also no ice; a cup of coffee no longer steaming; and an ashtray but no cigarette. The cigarette was tucked behind his ear. For a while she watched him, the typewriter's percussion faint like a far-off rattle of traffic over a metal bridge, the keystrokes coming in bursts and then pausing, before resuming again. Then he stopped, put his hands on his head, and stared up and out along the parallel walls of the two buildings – theirs and another – that made up Post Alley, over which the balcony looked. With the glass door closed it was like watching a silent film of some beautiful stranger, and she might've pretended then that she didn't know him.

Out on the balcony he looked off, deep in thought. The rain had stopped in the night and it was a bright morning, but water droplets still clung to the infinite green leaves of the ferns which grew from impossible ledges and cracks in the walls. Down the alley people walked on their way to the market and the sun reflected off the small, still puddles that adorned the dirty ground like pieces of a shattered mirror. In all of it he searched passively for the truth of things grand and small. He typed out a few more sentences, took a drink of water, another of whiskey, and then typed a bit more. After a while, he checked the watch on his wrist, measured the height of the sun in the sky, and rose to walk inside.

Do I know you? she asked from the bed as he opened the door and crossed the room, setting his glass on the bar cart. You never can tell anymore, he replied. Been taking pictures?

Without taking her eyes off him she made a noise like Mmm. Get any good ones? he asked, crossing the room again to sit on the bed beside her. She reached for the 35mm film camera on the bedside table and handed it to him. Look for yourself, she said.

He removed the lens cap, adjusted the exposure, and snapped two shots back-to-back, one of her smile with the sun in long wavy lines across her face, and the next with the covers pulled half-way over her head. The second he hoped would develop with a motion blur and still just a bit of her face visible amidst the movement.

How are we on film, he asked. From beneath the covers she mumbled something he couldn't understand. He yanked the duvet away exposing her body in the sunlight and asked, What?

She reached for the covers, but he caught her wrist and held it. Her eyes burned for a split second. I said that's the last role.

Thank you, he answered, relinquishing her wrist and his hold on the covers. She grabbed his shirt instead, though, and in pulling herself upright she also pulled him to her, and she kissed him briefly, passionately, before he stood. She looked at him, incredulous. I'm starving, he said.

I've got something you can eat. She leaned forward onto her arms, pressing her breasts together, biting her lip.

He swilled the remaining dregs of whiskey in his glass, downed them. You satiate my soul, he said. Not my stomach.

She was looking down at her breasts and said: Sorry girls – he doesn't want us anymore. We've lost our allure.

He took two steps toward her, lifted her chin with his thumb and forefinger, and kissed her mouth. Don't talk to them like that, he said.

Or what? You're going to punish me?

You'd like that, he replied, pulling on a white button down and beginning to work the buttons through their black surged holes.

When they exited onto the street, the bright sun on the freshly washed street made the old city feel new. They each looked in opposite directions, then looked at one another. She took his hand, he kissed the top of her head, and they set off walking.

Just seems like a waste
not to use every part of me
to ravage every part of you.

All these beautiful
dreams of home
and all along
it was just the space
between our hearts.

We started dancing
in the rain more often
because it wasn't fair
that whenever we were
together, she was the
only one getting wet.

I love you...

In case 10,000 poems
haven't made it
clear.

Is that the wind
whispering secrets
or has our love
opened portals
to the great beyond
again?

When I pin your hands
it's not because I don't
want you to touch me.

It's because I want you
to touch me with the
rest of your body.

The image of her
bent into a shape of my making
her body glowing like a whisper
in the dark and our silhouette
one animal with two hearts
burned into the walls of my memory.

It's Tuesday and all I've been able to do
is remember making love to her and the way
we turned that night of silvertone
and charcoal into a masterpiece of color
and movement.

She's the art that changed my eyes
the song that sewed the seeds of hope
into my pockets. The book that showed
me new ways to say 'I love you.'

J.P. Greene

My mouth misses
the parts of you
the rest of the world
never sees.

Look, she said
cradling her
broken wings.

Look how damaged
I've become.

No, I told her,
look at how much
you've survived
on the way to
becoming the person
you were always
meant to be.

She was strawberries
in summer and bluebird
skies in fall. The warmth
of a mug in-hand on a
snowy Sunday, and sweet
gentle rain in the dark
of a spring dawn.

She was everything good
about everything beautiful.

You know what they say
about too much
chocolate cake...

But you're not a cake
even though I do love
to eat you
and I'll never get tired
of the way you taste.

I never liked my name
until I heard you say it
and then I knew
what it meant
to be loved.

We danced
in the porch light
magic in the air
like fireflies
or snowflakes
but it was neither.

Just the twinkling
stardust of two souls
in love.

J.P. Greene

A picture worth
a thousand words,
her kiss easily
ten thousand poems.

Sitting here thinking
about you sitting
on my lap and my hands
running all over you
like a slow ride down
a mountain road.

J.P. Greene

The storm outside
thunder through the
summer dark
and every crack
of lightening
throwing shadows
of our bodies entwined
against every wall
painting this house
just for tonight
with all the things
we do to each other.

At lunch
daydreaming about
navigating the inside
of your thigh
finding high proof
of how much you want me
and suddenly
any hope of
any other thought
disappears
like smoke in the wind.

Wake with me into the
excruciating beauty
of the world knowing
what a risk it is
to love this much
and choosing to do it
anyway.

Your lips promised me
eternity, and for the
first time, I believed.

Lay with me
under the stars
so that heaven
can see clearly
what perfection
looks like.

I used to get so sad
waking up from
really beautiful dreams.

But now, with you,
the beautiful dreams
aren't confined to sleep.

In this mad world
where bad news
blooms like
dandelions
lips like yours
are good medicine.

Shadows of late
afternoon and the
delight of bodies
colliding and a
trace of kisses on
your neck and the
lovers' sleep of
utter contentment.

Like the first leaves
launching all the
world into autumn...

You ought to know,
that look
while you bite
your lip
is bound to set off
all manner of
beautiful colors
within me.

To sleep
wrapped in her arms
was the best way
he knew
to transform winter
into something
beautiful.

Simple love
uncomplicated by
scars, not because
we'd never been wounded
but because we were
each to the other
just the right
medicine.

Nights that leave us
breathless and weak
and mornings we
challenge the sun
for who can shine
brighter.

J.P. Greene

Finding you
was like unwrapping
a beautiful package
and finding pieces
of my own soul
inside.

Just these intrusive
thoughts of feeling
your hip bones pinned
between the wall
and my own.

Amber on every
secret inch of you,
streetlights through
the shades, and
not a single thread
of clothing to keep
your skin from mine.

VII

They were in a rented house in East Tennessee. It stood on the edge of a field delineated by a split rail fence and hemmed in by woods off in the distance. Autumn had stained everything auburn and gold.

He pointed the camera at her, squinted one eye, and stared through the viewfinder and she had to work very hard not to look at the way he drew up one corner of his mouth. Because if she looked at that she'd smile, and she didn't particularly want to be smiling in all her pictures. She much preferred to keep a serious and somewhat melancholy energy to the photographs, which was always some type of fun, artistic challenge because she often felt very happy around him.

It wasn't that she wanted to be portrayed as something other than what she was. It was just art.

It's awfully unfair, he said, adjusting the aperture, that I get to see you this way and you never do.

What are you talking about? she asked. I see the pictures. And there's mirrors, besides.

No, he said, his face still pressed to the camera's body. The photos don't ever even capture the half of it. I mean sure, the shadows and light maybe. Your body. But seeing you like this. It's more than that.

Someone's a little obsessed... she teased, turning so that she reclined on the sofa on one side, her body twisting in the most alluring way. She adjusted a bit of hair so that it fell half across her face.

More than a little, he replied, advancing the film with his thumb. The roll reached its end with a dull, half-drawn ratchet of the lever, and he dropped the camera away from his face, looking at her. But seriously, he said. What's not to be obsessed with? Have you met you?

She rolled her eyes but smiled. Kiss me, she said. He set the camera down on the coffee table that stood before the sofa and bent over her, his lips meeting hers in a stream of golden sunshine. Outside it was hazy and yellow and late evening, just before twilight and there was a stillness in the fields and the woods stretching out beyond the large windows of the living room. The light fell through the glass and gilded everything upon which it landed, most mesmerizingly her bare skin and the lace finery that hardly covered it.

I could do this until the day I die, he said, their lips still so close they brushed together as his mouth formed the words.

You better hope you die young, baby. I won't look like this forever.

He smiled, their lips still nearly touching, and said: To me you'll always be beautiful. And getting more so every day. He ran his forefinger beneath the strap of her bra and said, Now take this off for me. But let me reload first. I love the shots of you in motion. She smiled and watched as he stood and deftly wound the used film, swapped rolls, and threaded the new. In all it took him fifteen seconds. She drank it in as though it would last her a lifetime.

Okay, he said. Ready.

She rose and walked to the window, facing away from him, reached up behind her back and slowly unclasped the metal hook. Then she turned to face him, one shoulder strap falling down her arm, one arm crossed over her chest and positioned near her face, her thumb by her mouth. She bit her lip.

Don't move, he said. She did as told and held her pose. And then she let her bra drop and wove her fingers through her hair on top of her head. He snapped a half-dozen pictures of her like this and then looked around the room. For a brief moment he studied the light, looking every few seconds through the viewfinder at the meter readings, and then he told her to sit on one of the stools at the bar in the kitchen. As she crossed the room, she ran her fingers along the sheepskin draped over the back of the leather sofa and he captured a few frames that he expected to be overexposed because he hadn't had time to adjust. He got the feeling in his stomach that they would be his favorite few of all the hundred or so photographs they would take that day.

How do you want me? she asked as she came to the stool. In love with me, he replied, the camera once more against his face. Enzo, I'm serious, she said.

Fine, he answered. Turn it around – back toward the counter – and straddle it with your elbows on the bar. That's perfect.

Did I tell you Athena wants to shoot with us? she asked as he reloaded the camera again. He looked up at her briefly and shook his head. No, you didn't. Do you want to?

Of course, she's gorgeous. Don't you want to? I thought you liked her.

Be careful of your word choice there. I never said I liked her. But no, I wouldn't mind doing another shoot.

She invited us to some condo she has in Vail. Said we could come stay for the weekend. I imagine there will be some hot tubbing, some fun parties, some interesting people.

He paused, the camera now reloaded, and set it down on the bar. He came around the bar and stood behind her, his hands running down the curve of her back and coming to rest on her waist. His thumbs fit into the dimples at the very lowest part of her back. She sat up so that her shoulders pressed against his chest and reached her arms around behind his head. He kissed her just below the ear and she smiled.

Do you think it's wrong that neither of us ever gets jealous? he asked after a moment.

She inclined her neck just slightly to one side so that her cheek rested against his. Do I think it's wrong? No... Rare, yes... Are you worried?

He shook his head just slightly, his stubble rubbing against her face, and tightened his grip on her waist.

Look at us, she said, staring at the window glass where there existed the half-strength reflection of their bodies together.

He smiled. We won't look like this forever, he said.

She sighed. No, we won't. But we will feel like this forever won't we?

A silence grew between them for a moment as he kissed her neck and ran his hands over her bare skin. She arched herself against him even more. A silence of sound, but not of movement.

Yes, he said, his voice breathy and hardly audible except to the two of them. His eyes were closed, and he could smell her.

Do you love me? she asked, twisting around to look into his eyes.

And for a while he just stared into her, seeing not so much her eyes themselves as through them and into her being and feeling somehow that he was looking not only at her but also into himself and into a third thing that was neither her nor him but something instead which had been created by the two of them in love.

Or maybe what he saw was really just a girl in the loving gaze of a boy, and he thought then that that would be good enough.

More than life itself, he said.

What I can say
with so few words
is nothing compared
to what we can say
with just our two bodies
and no words at all.

Chemistry is cool
but have you ever met
someone fluent in
the very beating
of your heart?

I saw the moon tonight.

She asked how you've been.

Same as always
I told her.

Still out there
teaching all the stars
how to shine.

The shape of you
in candlelight and
moonbeams is my
favorite reminder
of God.

We have always been
far too great to
be contained in
just one life.

J.P. Greene

Yield to me in the dark
and I will move our two
bodies in such a way
that we become the light.

Promise me
you won't stop
dreaming just because
you woke up.

It's never been
a question of whether
I love you, but rather
how I might expand
my heart so that I
can feel all the things
inside me that you've
brought to life.

There is love
and then there's
the deep knowing
that I couldn't manage
a single full breath
if I didn't have you.
As though my life
would still go on
but it would never be
fully satisfying
ever again.

The secret truth
is I only lace my
fingers through
your hair and grab
so tightly
because my body
in that close proximity
to yours threatens
to slip away from
reality entirely.

Most kisses fade
like the ink from a
ballpoint pen
gone with soap and water.

But she stained my lips
and every inch of skin
and just like when
I got my first tattoo
I knew I was hooked
and that my body
would never be the same.

She fit into me
like a key
in a door I never
knew was locked
and so I stepped
out of myself
and found a freedom
I never knew
existed.

It might be
that it's the
dangerous parts
of you I love
the most.

Like fertile rain
upon my soul
your love made it
so that my heart
could once again
grow flowers and
other beautiful
blooming things.

Thing is
I knew I loved you
the moment I saw
your smile.

Three days was too long
to wait to call.

Three dates too long
to wait to kiss you
everywhere.

And even three seconds
was more than
it took to know
I would love you
forever.

We'll never be kids again
I thought as I watched
her cross the river
water wetting the cuffs
of her rolled-up jeans.

But it felt like we were
kids again and
would be forever.

At the end of the day
I'm glad you found
someone who makes you
so happy.

But selfishly
I'm really glad
that person is me.

Autumn
in early morning
when we lay in bed
warm in all the places
our bodies touch
listening to the city
awaken through open
windows that let in
the chill and the smell
and the damp dark of
shortening days
knowing that
as summer fades
our love
never will.

Petrichor:

The smell of rain on dry soil.

Or:

The feeling of your
skin on mine
after too long
apart.

There was sex
that brought out
his inner hedonist.

And then there was sex
that ripped him open
and let his heart
feel the sunshine
and the breeze
and the rain.

We can burn down
the house if it
makes you come
harder.

She was the perfect blend
of thrill and comfort
like the windows down
on a fall drive and
the heat blowing
on our feet.

Lips so soft
they could mend
a broken heart...

Woke up
to windows filled
with skies of blue
and dirty thoughts
of all the things
our lips can do.

Just like the creases
in the paper
and the half-strength
letters and all the
typos...

We are far from perfect
and it's these things
these imperfect things
that make us worth
loving.

VIII

When she woke up, he was writing. By the time she got out of bed, he was still at it, hunched over a page he'd just pulled from the Olivetti that had more cross-outs, margin notes and re-writes than originally typed letters. She went out for coffee with a friend of hers at one in the afternoon and kissed him on the neck, her fingers brushing across his shoulder, and he hardly pulled his eyes from what he was working on. Outside the rain made round, dark spots on the shoulders of her green canvas jacket.

When she came back in the early evening, she found him in the same place, his elbows on the desk, his head in his hands, his eyes glued to the page sticking out of the typewriter, a nearly empty bottle of whiskey within arm's reach. A glass with fingerprint smudges waited beside him, the dregs of amber liquor forgotten at the bottom. She watched him now and then from the kitchen as she cooked dinner for the two of them and narrowly resisted asking what he was working on.

Over dinner he stared vacantly at his pasta and spun it onto his fork, then let it slide off back onto the plate. She watched him, he looked up, smiled a half-hearted smile, and took a bite. Eventually she put down her fork and he looked up again, his eyes wide like someone who is lost and just realizing they don't know where they are.

Enzo, she said. What's going on?

He smiled as though to himself and nodded. Something seem off? he asked, looking toward the windows.

She stared at him, softening in spite of herself. It was a grey evening outside, and the rain fell and the light was soft and muted. There was a silence between them, like an item on the table, or like the essence of the table itself. She waited.

Today is the eighth of October.

Still, she waited.

It's been ten years since my mom died. Ten years ago, to the minute, I was sitting on my couch, and I still had a mother, and I was with my friends smoking weed, watching *Survivor*. And in – he looked at his watch – sixteen minutes, ten years ago, that stupid, scared kid checked his phone and saw a missed call from a local number, and a voicemail. And he laughed and tossed his phone and took another hit.

And in – Lorenzo checked his watch again – an hour and a half, as he sat on the toilet, that kid listened to his messages and found out, over the course of three voicemails, that his mom – his own mother – had overdosed, had been moved to the ICU, and had died.

Eleanore watched him. She reached across the table and put her hand on his arm, feeling a pang of gladness when he didn't pull away.

And I sat on the toilet feeling more vulnerable and exposed than I ever had in my entire life. I stayed in there so long my buddies made fun of me because they thought I'd fallen asleep.

He'd put his silverware down. His elbows were on the table. He stared at a smudge on his glass as though it was an anchor that might somehow keep him from drifting away. He drew a breath and let it out. The rain picked up outside and she glanced to the windows and then back to him.

There's nothing you could've done, she said.

He pressed his lips together in the semblance of a smile, which fell quickly after, like a bird shot just after taking flight, and looked down at his lap. He ran his free hand through his hair, the other hand now cradled in both of hers across the table. I know, he said after a while. He said it so quietly it was hardly more than a whisper.

Do you? Really?

He nodded. But even still she didn't believe him.

Lorenzo.

He looked at her. And she saw into his eyes and down into the depth of his heart. And in that moment the hand she held across the table was not a man's hand but a little boy's.

Tell me about her, she said.

He stared back into her eyes. Like he was looking for permission. Or looking for a home he hoped to find. Can we go to bed?

She nodded and thought the conversation was finished. But ten minutes later as they lay in bed with the streetlight casting burnt orange shapes onto the far walls of the room and the rain beating codes on the window glass – as she held him and he lay in on her chest with both his arms wrapped around her waist – he said: She tried so hard.

Eleanore waited, staring up at the trussed industrial ceiling and stroking his hair.

My old man was gone before I was born. He was killed in a work accident when my mom was six months pregnant. She got a big pay-out from the company. So we didn't have to worry about money, but she worried about me. For as long as I can remember she's been worried about me.

Eleanore waited and listened, feeling the way her heartbeat moved the bones of his face with each pulse, astonished by how very close they were in that moment.

He was silent for a while. The rain fell outside and the cars going by made sounds like static on an old radio. She wondered if he was falling asleep. And then he said: When I was eight or nine, she started having back pain. They gave her pills for the pain. It wasn't a smart thing to do. They just gave them to her like they were aspirin or something.

For a while she hid it from me. But I found out. I didn't really get it till I started seeing friends get hooked on the same things – pills mostly – and then I started to piece it together. About my mom, I mean. Some of my friends moved on to heroin. I was the only one not getting tied up. We'd smoke weed, but I never... he trailed off. Then he drew a breath and closed his eyes, and she held him closer.

She was a good mom, you know. She really— She really tried. I found out after she died – at the funeral actually – that she'd been going to NA. Her sponsor felt like I deserved to know she was trying to get clean. All it did was make me feel like I should've known.

Eleanore started to speak but stopped herself, the breath half-filling her chest, escaping unused as a heavy exhale instead.

Or like I'd pushed her somehow, like she wouldn't have needed to run away if I'd been a better son. I know it's not true. In my mind I know it. But there are parts of me that don't know it.

She told him then to lay on his back, and she climbed on top of him. Tell me what parts of you don't know it, she said.

He stared at her in the dark, her shape an amber silhouette against the dark room and her eyes like a cat's, or like lighthouses. I don't know, he said.

So she leaned down and kissed his forehead and ran her hand through his hair. And then she kissed his collarbone and the ridge of his cheek and then she kissed his lips and paused, their lips touching and motionless, the two of them sharing, it seemed, one singular breath, and then she kissed his chest, right in the middle, on his sternum. It's not your fault, she whispered to his skin after each kiss she gave. And her hands held him all the while, and he lay there, and it felt as though she were unraveling knots that had been tight and hard and unworkable for so many years. She wasn't speaking to be heard by his ears. She spoke into him, in order to be felt by his bones and his muscles and all the parts of him that still didn't believe in forgiveness. And all the while it felt to him as though he was witnessing some divine consecration of this body in which he'd lived his whole life, but was just now being welcomed home to.

When she was finished, she crawled up beside him and pulled the covers snugly over the two of them, and she lay down in the bend of his arm the way she always did, and rested her leg overtop of his. And then they slept.

She never held me
so tightly that I
couldn't leave
and it was this
more than anything
that made me want
to stay.

I met you
and learned to smile.

And after the
first night
I knew
I would never sleep
again.

After, we lie together
and the tides recede
and our fingers wander
and our breathing slows.
But our hearts never
stop making love.

Take me anywhere
in the entire world
and I'll never feel
better than when
I'm in your arms.

Breathe in
I said, and then
I filled her
the rest of the way.

Sing me your
Saturday morning songs
while I make us coffee
and the sun streams
through the windows
in ribbons of gold
like it's desperate
to take part in the
permanent magic
of us.

All these words
I want to say
and still
she'd rather use
my mouth
for kissing.

I'm convinced there's more
than mind to memories.

Because my skin remembers
every place you've touched me
and my lips remember every
single time I've whispered
your name and there's a permanent
dent in my heart from where
it collided with yours.

She waterproofed me
and from then on
all the rain of
hard and nasty things
rolled off my shoulders
and I didn't even
notice.

I just went on smiling
at her all the while.

Dark shadows of animal loving
carnivorous passion in waves
our limbs and inhibitions
scattered on the porch
our clothes strewn
down the hall
and all of me
inseparable
from all
of you.

Outside, a silver tone scratchwork
of branches and ice
all moonlit and moving
in a nightwind.

And inside, you in my arms
and both of us
safe and held and warm.

And all is fine
in the world.

To me
you hung the stars
which is to say
you took my darkest nights
and made them beautiful.

I don't need to shout
my love for you from
the mountain tops.

I just want to whisper
it directly into your skin
so it reaches the soft
dark of every doubt you've
ever had.

The first time I saw you
you looked at me like
we'd already met
a thousand times.

That was when I realized
that time doesn't follow
the same set of rules
where love is concerned.

I said to her
you are my sun
meaning my horizons
could shift daily
with life unfurling
showing all the ways
I have yet to live
and still you will
always be the
brightest light
in my sky.

J.P. Greene

They say you can hear
the ocean inside any
seashell you find.

I wonder if
when someone listens
to my heart
they can hear your voice.

Love me so fiercely
even the gods know
they don't stand
a chance at
keeping us
apart.

Everyone knows
I started glowing
more brightly
after we met.

The way we dance
our words, bodies,
lips, fingers,
all of us set to music
and moving as one
and every dip and sway
choreographed to a
music only we
can hear.

She made me nostalgic
for a love I never had.

One that smelled
like high tide and
shook like horsepower
between your legs
pulsing with all the freedom
of the California
summer of 1969.

And then I realized
that what I love most
about every beautiful thing
I've ever seen is that
it reminds me
of you.

J.P. Greene

I think the moon
blushes when you
look at her
as though it's you
and not the sun
who makes her shine.

In the place where
words never go –
in that magical
ineffable wilderness.

Let's live there
forever.

When I go
I hope to be
drunk on you
and writing poems
only we
understand.

IX

When they got home from the party she walked through the door, leaving it open behind her, and dropped her things on the floor as she made her way directly to the bedroom.

Eleanore, he said after her. What's going on? Are you feeling okay?

Fine, she said. I have a headache. I'm going to bed.

Can I get you anything?

No, it's fine.

Eleanore, he repeated, grabbing her arm and turning her to face him. At first she avoided his eyes but eventually she met them. He could see in her the scared animal of past hurt threatening to come back alive, and he tried as best as he could to keep it at bay. And then he knew what was taking place within her, and he said: This is about Hailey.

No, she said, averting her eyes and pulling away. She turned toward the bed and began to take off her dress, sliding her arms out of the straps and shimmying it down over her hips. He watched her and it occurred to him how important the context of love was to the awakening of desire. How he could watch her undress and love her without a single hesitation and yet, in that moment fraught with unspoken wounds, there was nothing sexual about her nakedness. How it was his heart that he wanted to give her in that moment of her vulnerability, and not his body.

He walked up behind her and put his hands on her hips. She froze, as though his touch was something to guard against, but she didn't push him away. He held her waist and he spoke quietly and he told her that they didn't need to talk about it right then if she didn't want to, but that he was there to listen to her whenever she was ready. He could feel in the electricity of her spine that she relaxed just slightly and he took a quarter step closer so that only an inch of space remained between their bodies. Then, as though drawn by some invisible force, she eased toward him so that her bare skin pressed against the soft fabric of his pants and shirt, and his hands drifted forward to hold her stomach. She leaned her head back against his shoulder and he kissed her behind the ear.

I'm tired baby, she said. He nodded, his face against the hair that fell on her neck, but didn't answer.

Are you sure you don't still love her?

No, he said.

She turned toward him and studied his face, expecting to see shame or regret or deliverance or surrender to the tides of the kind of feelings people try to stifle and fail. But instead, she saw his presence, his eyes staring back at hers clear and open and she knew then that he wasn't finished talking.

I think once we love we never stop loving.

She watched his mouth and his eyes in alternating glances. He reached for her wrists and put her hands on his shoulders as though they were slow dancing.

I do still love her. I love the person she is and the person I became because of the all the ways she and I will never work.

But what if she changes? Eleanore asked. There were tears threatening the corners of her eyes.

She could. Some people do. But I've also changed.

He returned his hands to her waist.

I've changed, he went on, in ways that make it so that she's not what I want or need anymore.

And what do you want and need now?

You, he said.

The gravity of that single word took up every inch of space in the room.

I hate that you always know just what to say, she said after a moment, but she was smiling in spite of herself and glancing to the side.

I have only ever told you the truth, he replied.

An ambulance went by outside and the lights cascaded into the room and then faded, like a brief, manic hallucination, and he watched as the light enlivened her eyes.

Why do I find it so easy to believe you? She slapped his chest.

Maybe you're just a trusting person, he suggested.

No, she said, slipping forward towards him so that her hips pressed against his and her forearms rested on his shoulders, her arms crossed at the wrist behind his head.

Well, I don't know. It's like maybe you feel safe or something.

I do, she said.

I like that.

I like it, too.

I like you.

She smiled.

I love you, Eleanore. And I will forever.

But what if we change and I'm not what you want?

Maybe, he said. But maybe the best things never end after all. And we just go on forever in love.

That's a beautiful thought.

So are we, he said after a moment.

We are, aren't we?

Maybe the world
never ends
and we just go on
forever in love.

Epilogue

The years had been kind until they hadn't. It had been a long time since Eleanore had been able to wash her own hair or make her own breakfast or drive herself anywhere. At first it happened little by little and Lorenzo found it endearing that she would sometimes stop in the middle of a task and look up like she had just come out of a dream. But one day the police had called in the middle of the morning in January because they'd found her crying at the bus station and when someone had asked if she was alright she hadn't been able to tell them her name or her address or really anything about herself except that she was trying to get to Seattle to meet a man she'd once fallen in love with on a balcony in the rain. When Lorenzo picked her up she didn't recognize him.

So year by year he clung to whatever threads of her memory that seemed so tenuously to remain and he hoped against all odds that he would remain lucid enough himself to continue to be the one to care for her. They'd never had children.

It was one of those dim winter evenings that feels like a long sad farewell and seems not to move at all until all at once it's over. Eleanore was sitting in her favorite golden embroidered channel back chair listening to records that Lorenzo had stacked on the automatic turntable for her, and looking out the window at the forlorn cape of yellow-orange that fell from the streetlight. Lorenzo sat at his writing desk in the next room looking at old polaroids. At some point he became aware of motion in the hallway and realized that she had stood and was now making her way around the small house. He could hear the soft brush of her slippers on the wooden floor and he approximated what she might be doing.

For a while he followed her through the house by her footsteps and wondered as he now so often did what she might be thinking, or if she was thinking anything at all. The footsteps would sound and then pause, sound and pause, and he listened on. When they had not sounded in what began to feel like a long time, he pushed back his chair and walked to the hallway to see what she was doing. He found her staring at a framed poem that hung halfway down the hall and when his shadow darkened the doorway to the kitchen she turned to face him looking more aware than usual. He smiled at her and she smiled back and for a moment it was like she had returned.

He must've loved her, she said, her gaze returning to the poem. He still does, he replied.

Something akin to hope flashed behind her eyes and she said something like she was glad that they were still alive and in love. Lorenzo took the few steps to close the gap between them and placed his hand on her back right beneath the place her wings would've been if she had them. She leaned her head against his shoulder and signed.

Who wrote this? she asked after a moment. Lorenzo smiled and said that he had written it.

She smiled, too – he knew she was smiling, but he could not have said how he knew. To have lived this kind of love, she said. Who is it about?

You, he said simply.

She picked her head up off his shoulder and looked at him and for just the briefest of fleeting moments she looked into him and he into her and they once again saw each other for who they had been.

Pay attention old boy, he told himself. This is what it's like. Driving through the forest, the sun peaking through the trees in flashes so fast you wonder if they ever happened. Don't forget to love her while she's here. And she wrapped her arms around his neck and rested her head on his chest and he held her. Are there more? she asked. More poems?

Hundreds, he said.

Can I see them?

At the kitchen table they sat side by side with an old suitcase open on the table between them. Inside were innumerable scraps of paper of all different sorts, some with ink so faded it was almost impossible to read but for the typewriter's indentations. Her face was shaped as though she was on the very cusp of overwhelm and her eyes glistened. These are all about me, she said. Lorenzo smiled at her and squeezed the fingers of her left hand.

Will you read them to me? she asked. Start at the beginning.

the end

(is never really the end)

J.P. Greene is the author of two other novels:

The Arid Road Home
2022 Wilderwest Press

The Beauty of Sadness
2024 Word Rebels Press

Learn more about the author at
www.TypewrittenLoveNotes.com
or on Instagram:

@TypewrittenLoveNotes

ACKNOWLEDGEMENTS

This book would not be possible without the support, encouragement, and editorial contributions of so many people. First, I would like to thank my family – David, Donna, Jonah, and Tara, for their unyielding love and belief in me, and for teaching me how to love. I would not be who I am without my kids – Esme and Indra and Xander – y'all are the best thing ever to happen to me and I will love you forever. To the multitudes of people I've met along my journey, but especially to Meredith, thank you for the ways you've helped me make this book what it is. To Claire G for helping put this book on the map. To Taylor N for curating the most incredible playlist. And even though she'll never read this, to D. for the innumerable ways she informed these characters.

An excerpt from

The Beauty of Sadness
A novel by J.P. Greene

I

Jake Barnes had the only apartment on Main Street with a balcony. And though it wasn't large – a few feet deep and maybe ten feet wide – it was the balcony itself that had made him certain he wanted the apartment in the first place. Up the two flights of stairs, the landlord had fumbled with the keys, opened the front door, led him through into the kitchen. Jake looked across the open floor to the living area and saw the French doors opening outward to the iron railing around the small platform. The smell of old buildings. Plaster and worn pine floors refinished in heavy varnish and then worn down once again. A gas stove and a porcelain sink. Tile in the kitchen. A white enameled radiator in the living room beneath one of the long, tall windows. The block had been built in 1901.

The sun ran in bright torrents through the windows painting tangerine trapezoids on the yellow plaster wall. An air of calm. He put his hands in his pockets and said he'd take it. Plenty of light, he thought. The plants will be happy.

The landlord seemed surprised. He'd only shown the first room.

It's okay, Jake said, I want it. I'm certain. He pulled cash from his pocket and began counting hundreds. He looked up smiling. Can I move in this afternoon? It was the peak of summer. The middle of July.

The man looked around as though to verify that it was in fact vacant and then shrugged his shoulders in agreement.

The next day, in the high afternoon, Jake sat on an orange fabric sofa with his feet propped up on a woven cane ottoman, one crossed over the other. The balcony doors were open, the breeze blowing in gently and rustling the pages of a paperback that sat on the side table. He listened to the sounds below, traffic and laughter, and from somewhere else in the building a faint music. The sun slanted across the room catching all the dust that still hung from moving in. He rose from the sofa and walked to the kitchen and selected a peach from a clay bowl on the table. He admired its impossibly bright, cheery color before rinsing it in the sink. He then patted it dry with a dish towel and walked to the balcony to eat. The juice of it ran down his forearm and dripped off his elbow making little dark circles on the balcony's concrete floor, which would quickly become sticky in the sun. A bee buzzed in through the iron railing and landed at one of the drops, drinking for a moment before buzzing off drunkenly. He watched and raised his half-eaten peach in a sort of salute as it flew away. The sweetness of the fruit pulled the muscles in his jaw tight and he smiled at the sensation. The soft fuzz of the skin against his lips as he bit. The yielding richness of the supple flesh. The cool of it against the heat of the sun. A car honked. He craned his neck upward to see the position of the sun relative to himself, and saw that in an hour or two it would have crossed beyond the roofline, and then shade would come into the apartment. He looked inside from the balcony, the peach now a pit in his hand held easily between his thumb and forefinger, and admired the stillness of his new home.

There was not much that he'd needed to unpack, because he owned very little, except for plants. More of them than he cared to count. There was the sofa, an old record player in its original beechwood case that sat atop an arrangement of milk crates filled with records. A few kitchen implements, an old clay vessel filled with wooden spoons, the candy-red Dutch oven that would live, mostly, on the stovetop. There stood a table in the kitchen; a thin, hardwood oval atop narrow, tapered wooden legs with brass cuffs at the bottom. Chairs to match.

He'd mounted a coatrack in the entry with a shelf on top that held three or four of the innumerable plants. In his room, a simple wooden platform bed, its legs tapered wood that matched the table, stained in the same dark mahogany color. A circular mirror that hung on the back of the bedroom door. Then there was the cane-woven ottoman that occupied a space somewhere in front of the sofa, and a shaggy, woolen rug. And then the plants that took over every nook and corner. No space devoid of life, it seemed, and a simple stillness lent by the very presence of them.

There was one plant he loved possibly more than all the others. An overbearing monstera that climbed its way out of an enormous clay pot and occupied the majority of the corner beside the balcony's French doors. Its leaves extended at least five feet in every direction, the leaves themselves larger than dinner plates, their fenestrations giving the thing a carefree, almost lazy look. From his place on the balcony he could see a new leaf emerging from a high stem, its tightly coiled new flesh still bright green and waiting to unfurl. Two more days and it would be dangling from its stem, neon and limp like wet paper in a new world. All new things come into the world vulnerably, he thought.

He looked down below and saw the people walking. The shadow of the building opposite crept across the street like a closing door. He moved inside, leaving the balcony doors open, tossing the peach pit into the sink from across the room. He walked into his bedroom and took a soft, linen button-down from a hanger in his closet and pulled it on. The fabric was soft and cool on his skin still warm from the sun. He maneuvered the surged buttonholes around the wooden buttons with a sort of mindless reverence typical of still, summer afternoons and then adjusted the way it hung off his shoulders. He grabbed his book from the side table. By the door he kept a pair of leather sandals, and on his way out he slid them on.

He left without locking up. In the hallway he passed an open door through which he could hear someone singing and vacuuming, the sounds and smells of the street outside drifting even to the hallway. Everyone with their windows open, a gift of old buildings without air conditioning.

He descended the steps lightly and emerged onto the street. He paused, his eyes adjusting to the brightness and looked left, then began to walk to the right. The movement felt good in his legs and he looked into the windows of the shops as he went, eventually reaching a small pedestrian alley between buildings that would lead him after a time to the market square. The stone and brick of the buildings on either side lent a coolness to the alleyway and he savored the change in temperature. There were a few delivery doors open to restaurant kitchens and the smells of their wares drifted out to meet him. A cat leaped from a ledge on his approach and disappeared into a shadow. A couple walked ahead very close together, laughing conspiratorially.

He came to the plaza and once again to the bright heat. There was a fountain that sprang from the center and another couple sat on the edge talking very closely and smiling at one another. It was a big fountain, with a concrete edging that went all the way around where people could sit. Beside it, the moving water cooled the air and it was a very pleasant place to be, so Jake chose a spot somewhere opposite the couple and situated himself to read. After a while a child approached and leaned over the edge a few feet away from Jake, his chubby hand reaching for the water, which his short, round fingers could barely graze. He wiggled closer so that he could submerge his palm.

Careful there Nico, a voice said. A woman – presumably the boy's mother – was approaching in no particular hurry, an easy contentment illuminating her face. Jake looked up at her from his spot and she smiled. He went back to reading and the woman sat down on the other side of her son, watching him explore the water. The boy and his mother talked idly but Jake didn't listen to their conversation.

After a time the boy began sloshing the water side to side, making a small wave with his hand, slapping at it and giggling when the droplets burst upward from the surface. One of these splashes landed a few drops on the pages of Jake's book, and the woman, having seen what happened, reached for her son and apologized automatically.

Jake was chuckling. Not to worry, he said. I'm asking for it anyway, sitting here like this. The woman relaxed. He went back to reading.

Momma feel the water, the boy was saying. The woman reached down and let her fingers brush the irregular surface. Mm, she said. It's so cool! It's so wet! the boy exclaimed. Jake couldn't help but chuckle again, and he glanced at the woman and found her also laughing, her face bright and relaxed, and in the midst of their shared levity they smiled at one another with their eyes as much as with their mouths.

After a while, the boy and his mother moved on and Jake remained alone on the edge of the fountain. He was passively aware of them as they moved around the square, looking at the sculpture installations in some of the flower beds, or climbing the stairs of the public stage at one end of the plaza. Once, Jake looked up at the sound of her voice carrying more loudly across the open space.

Oh my goodness! she exclaimed. It's so beautiful! The boy was holding out a flower with a broken stem that he had clearly picked for her, an enormous, proud grin across his face. She took it and pinched the broken stem off just below the flower's base, and put it behind her ear. Like this? she said, spinning on her toes. The boy cackled a boundless laugh and then found himself scooped up, his mother's face buried in his neck as he laughed and wiggled to get free.

It wasn't until the mother looked up, her eyes meeting his, that Jake realized he'd been staring. She held his gaze for a moment, her eyes seeming to resist pulling away. He became distracted by an argument across the way in which a woman was upset by something her boyfriend had done. He watched closely until she stormed off and the man, lost to perplexity, looked around with a defeated embarrassment. When Jake returned his attention to where the woman and the child had been, they were gone. He sat for a while longer.

When he rose, he dusted the backs of his pants and made his way across the plaza to the bakery.

On his way back to his apartment, the sun lower now and some of the heat lessening along with it, he passed a fruit and vegetable seller that was set up on the corner out front of a closed-up restaurant. From the stand he bought two large, deep purple heirloom tomatoes and a few stems of fresh basil. Then he looped around to Pinon Street to get some cheese from a small specialty shop. He asked if they sold wine but the cashier said that they didn't. His arms were already full with the produce and the bread and now the cheese, so he went home.

He surveyed his purchases spread out on the kitchen counter. The baguette, the tomatoes, the lump of fresh mozzarella in its small square of linen cloth. It needs wine, he thought. He left these items arranged haphazardly in the late golden sunlight like some still-life painting, and walked back down the stairs and along the street to a stall where an old man sat on a stool from two in the afternoon until two in the morning selling bottles of cheap wine. He walked in and scanned the crates of bottles. There was another man who was stocking the few shelves from boxes on the ground, and as Jake looked, the man asked if he could help him find anything.

Looking for a malbec, Jake said. Do you have any you recommend?

The man smiled, pulled a bottle with a tan paper label and handed it to him, looking at Jake over the glasses perched low on his nose. Toscana, he said. Full body, sharp and a little spicy. I prefer it to a malbec any day. He grinned beneath a thick, black moustache. Jake was about to ask if they didn't have any malbec, but decided instead to take his word for it, thanked him, paid the old man at the front, and walked the half block back to his apartment.

Inside the shop directly below, the woman and her young son were enjoying an ice cream cone. Most of it had melted across the boy's face and he happily, though unsuccessfully, licked at the soggy cone while she smiled and laughed at his enthusiasm. Jake didn't see them, but the mother saw him cross outside the shop windows and turn into the next doorway.

Upstairs, Jake sliced the baguette, the cheese and one of the tomatoes, then assembled the slices into stacks and lightly salted and peppered them. He pinched off a few leaves of basil and put them over top of the slices of mozzarella, and arranged them on a small plate, sniffing his fingers after and savoring the basil's lingering aroma. He tasted a slice of tomato with salt and nodded to himself, even though they weren't quite as good as the ones he got from Marty at the weekly farmer's market.

He poured some of the wine into a long-stem glass and made his way to the balcony. The doors were still open, as he'd left them. He paused half-way through the living room, looked back into the kitchen, and set the plate and glass of wine down on the cane ottoman. Then he crossed back to the kitchen and grabbed one of the chairs, which he set down on the small balcony, its back against one side at a slight angle, so that he could prop his feet up on the front railing. Before he resumed his migration, he pulled an Édith Piaf record from its sleeve and placed it on the turntable. He pressed the large, square power button and the speed indicator light illuminated as the table began to spin. Just as he was resting the needle down, there arose a child's shrieking cry from somewhere on the street. He moved to the balcony and looked down to see the woman holding the boy closely to her chest. He could see, even from the third story, a trickle of blood crawling down the boy's leg.

Without really thinking very much about it, he moved quickly out his door and down the two flights of stairs to the street entrance, where he emerged directly in front of the woman, who was still crouching and holding her child. People looked as they walked by, but none stopped and none offered help. As the door closed behind him the mother looked up and her expression changed from one of tired compassion to one of almost baffled amusement. He smiled and, without thinking, knelt down.

That's quite a scrape there, he said, still smiling.

The toddler turned suddenly to look toward the stranger's voice, his sobbing temporarily interrupted by his own curiosity. He watched Jake's face for a suspended moment before sniffling into his mother's collar.

I'm a firefighter. I live right here – if you can hold tight just a few minutes, I can run upstairs and get my things, and we can get that leg cleaned up and bandaged. Let me just get a wet cloth and I'll be right back down. I have a few magic band-aids left, I think. He started to turn but the mother said, Would it be easier if we just... came up?

Jake paused to look at her, then smiled and said, Sure, yeah. That would be great.

It's a few flights of stairs, I'm afraid, Jake said as he led them inside. His voice echoed slightly against the stairwell's plastered walls.

Good thing you've got a strong momma, the mother said to her son, playfully. The boy did not laugh.

I'm sorry, the woman said then, I didn't mean to invite ourselves in like that. How rude of me.

No, no, Jake responded quickly. You're right – this does make much more sense.

He led them into his apartment and pulled out a kitchen chair for them. Then he found a clean cloth in the drawer and ran some cool water over it, wrung it out, and handed it to the woman who took it and smiled up at him from where she knelt on the floor in front of the boy. Wait here, he said as he ducked into his bedroom to retrieve the first aid kit he always carried on his wildland fire assignments.

When he came back, she had wiped the blood from the child's leg and, though his bottom lip still trembled, he had stopped crying. Jake could see, even without looking closely, that it was hardly more than a small scrape.

Okay, big guy, let's see here, he said, kneeling down beside the boy's mother and unzipping the kit. What happened to your leg? Shark attack? Dinosaur race? Oh, wait – don't tell me. You were swinging from the buildings like spiderman and your web broke?

The boy chuckled. The woman beamed.

No! The boy said. I was trying to change into a bufferfly but the magic didn't work and I turned into a fish istead!

Wow! Jake said. That's the craziest thing I've ever heard! Is that really what happened?

The boy suddenly grew sullen again and looked down at his legs. I was running and I fell down. His lip started to tremble. His mother placed her hand on his unwounded knee. Jake glanced at her bare ring finger.

Ah, I hate when that happens, he said. It's okay, I have these magic band-aids here. These are official firefighter band-aids. The boy continued frowning but nodded.

First, he went on, we're going to put some of this magic cream (he showed the tube of Neosporin to the boy's mother and she nodded). The boy pulled his knee away.

Oh, don't worry, this won't hurt. It's magic, remember? The boy tentatively offered his knee.

Jake applied the cream and then carefully placed a band-aid over the small scrape, the boy's chubby knee yielding under the pressure of his thumbs on the bandage.

What do we think, Mom? Jake asked. Does that look about fixed up to you?

Her lips seemed all the time to hold the premonition of a smile and the seriousness of observation. She looked to her son, at his knee, then back to Jake. I think it looks perfectly perfect, she said. The corners of her mouth drew up just slightly, but her eyes shone.

She always says that, the boy said.

I like it, Jake responded.

Do you have any snacks? the boy asked.

Oh, Nico, she said, suddenly blushing. That's not polite. This man has been so kind and generous to—

Actually, Jake said interjecting, I do.

Oh, you don't have to do tha—

Have you ever eaten a rising star? Jake asked the boy, whose eyes went wide.

Now, it's not a real star, I should tell you. It's a kind of peach called a rising star. But it's the greatest thing you've ever had. Would you like to try one?

The boy nodded, grinning excitedly. Jake turned to his mother: Is that okay, Mom?

Call me Chase, she said, extending her hand. And yes, that's very kind of you. Her eyes fluttered.

Jake, he said, taking her hand in his. Her skin felt impossibly soft.

He rose to standing and sliced up one of the peaches, plated it and set it down on the table as Chase spun the boy's chair around.

I don't mean to be inappropriate, Jake began, but would you like a glass of wine? I don't know if it's any good but we can find out together?

I'd like that, Chase said.

Jake nodded and crossed into the living room to retrieve the wine and bruschetta which still sat on the cane ottoman. The record had run out and was skipping on its groove. He flipped it and set the needle down and music bloomed softly from the speakers. When he came back, he set the plate on the table between Chase and himself, then turned to fetch the bottle and another glass. He poured her a shallow pour and they toasted to their successful rescue. Her face was warm and relaxed.

I love all your plants, she said looking around. How do you keep them all alive?

Leprechauns, he said. A whole band of them who live in my baseboards who come out every night and tend to the plants. He gesticulated grandly.

Nico's eyes widened and he asked if Jake was really serious.

Oh, I wouldn't joke about something like that, he said in response.

The boy watched Jake, his eyes still wide, his expression very serious.

You've been very generous, Chase said after a few bites.

It's nothing – Actually, you two are my first guests in this new apartment.

No way! Chase said looking around. When did you move in? It all seems so settled already.

Yesterday, Jake said, washing down his last bite with a swig of wine. She looked at him, awaiting a punchline.

No, I'm serious, he said, noticing her still watching him. As you can see I'm a bit of a minimalist – moving in was a quick affair.

Nico was enjoying his slices of peach with genuine enthusiasm, the yellow, sticky juice in small explosions on each of his soft, round cheeks. His plump fingers and hands sticky to the wrists. We live in a basement, he said casually.

That's cool, Jake said. Like a secret lair. How's that rising star?

The boy looked up with a wry grin, still chewing, but said nothing.

Looks like approval to me, Chase said. The boy nodded emphatically.

So you're a firefighter, she asked. Here in town?

Jake shook his head and swallowed. No – only during the fire season. I work wildland crews during the summer and fall. Every once in a while I'll get a call during the winter months. But mostly it's a summer and fall gig.

I've never met a firefighter before, she said, picking up a stack of bruschetta and eyeing him with a look of intrigue. Possibly interest. Do you enjoy it?

Jake chuckled, avoiding her eyes. I'm not sure I do enjoy it. But I need to do it. Something about it that feels necessary to my life. I took a year off and something important vanished for me. It's hard, and hot, and endless seeming. Most of the time anyway. But as soon as I'm off for a week, I'm counting the days until I get back out there. Besides, the people I work with are some of the greatest in the world. He was leaning easily back in his chair now, one arm resting up on the chair's back, the other holding his wine glass.

She nodded. Have you already been out this year?

I have – I'm on a two-week break right now. We just finished out in California last week. I hear we may be going to Idaho next. Or staying here in Colorado. Depends on how a few of these smaller fires change in the next few days.

It sounds like quite an adventure, she said.

Nico was finishing his peach and was looking like he might be about to shimmy down from the table. Chase rose and wetted the cloth she'd used to clean his knee, using an unsoiled corner to wipe his face and hands. He squirmed against her but she expertly held his wiggling body and successfully removed the majority of the residual juice.

When she released him he asked Jake if he had any toys.

She was about to interject again, but Jake looked around, then rose from the table and pulled out an assortment of pots, a colander and a cheese grater. He walked to the living room and arranged them in a semicircle on the rug while Nico looked on with curious interest. Then he went back into the kitchen, returning a moment later with two wooden spoons.

Okay, you sit here, he said, indicating the space in the middle of the overturned pots. Nico did as asked. And now you just—

He banged on a few of the pots with the round side of the spoons, and then offered them to the boy.

Nico looked at his mother briefly before banging the side of the colander and then the edge of one the pots. A grin spread across his face. Jake lifted the needle on the record and was about to turn off the player, but Nico turned around fiercely and told him to put it back on so he could play along.

I've got something better, Jake said, chuckling. He replaced the Édith Piaf record with Led Zeppelin and set the needle down on Whole Lotta Love.

For the next forty minutes Nico banged along to both sides of the record, smiling and moving his little body all around to the music while Chase and Jake sat in the kitchen and talked. They had to sit very close to each other in order to hear over the din of the make-shift drums, and a few times she touched his leg beneath the table as she laughed at something he'd said. He could smell her and he thought she smelled like home in some inexplicable way. A mix of magnolias and amber. Once, a strand of hair fell beside her mouth and Jake tucked it back behind her ear without meaning the gesture to be so intimate. She smiled at him as he did it and turned her face slightly so it rested against his hand. He kissed her briefly, but stopped. She bit her lip and blinked quickly. It was only when he went to top off her glass that they realized they'd finished the whole bottle of wine.

Outside, the light had shifted and the clock on the stove read six-thirty. When the record ran out again Chase said they should be going. Nico protested but she reminded him it was bath night. At first he crossed his arms and said he was never taking a bath again, but he relented when she said they could put extra bubbles.

As they assembled themselves to walk down the steps, she was about to thank Jake again for his generosity, but he said he'd walk them out.

As he exited behind them he paused and ran back inside, grabbing the bag of peaches, which he had decided he would give to Nico.

Out on the street Chase stood looking up at him for a few moments longer than necessary, and he felt the strong desire to pull her to him but didn't. He broke her gaze and offered the bag of peaches to Nico, who took them excitedly and, without prompting, hugged Jake's leg and said thanks for the rising stars.

As this happened Jake looked back to Chase, who appeared softened by the boy's act of affection. Well, he said, maybe I'll see you around. She reached down and scooped up the boy. As they walked away, she turned her head and winked at Jake. If you're lucky, she said. And again he thought to himself, all new things come into the world vulnerably.

Learn more about the author at
www.TypewrittenLoveNotes.com
or on Instagram:

@TypewrittenLoveNotes

www.ingramcontent.com/pod-product-compliance
Lightning Source LLC
Chambersburg PA
CBHW011851300726
48970CB00009B/2745